ONE SMALL BLUE BEAD

for David Baylor

— B.B.

Second edition published by Charles Scribner's Sons 1992

Text copyright ©1965 by Byrd Baylor Schweitzer
Illustrations copyright ©1992 by Ronald Himler

Charles Scribner's Sons Books for Young Readers
Macmillan Publishing Company
866 Third Avenue, New York, NY 10022

Maxwell Macmillan Canada, Inc.
1200 Eglinton Avenue East, Suite 200
Don Mills, Ontario M3C 3N1

Macmillan Publishing Company is part of the
Maxwell Communication Group of Companies.

Printed in the United States of America
10 9 8 7 6 5 4 3 2 1

Library of Congress Cataloging-in-Publication Data
Baylor, Byrd.
One small blue bead / Byrd Baylor ;
pictures by Ronald Himler.   p.   cm.
Summary: A boy makes it possible for an old man in their primitive tribe to go in search of other men in far-off places.
ISBN 0-684-19334-5
[1. Man, Prehistoric—Fiction.   2. Stories in rhyme.]
I. Himler, Ronald, ill.   II. Title.
PZ8.3.B348On   1992   [Fic]—dc20   90-28160

ONE SMALL BLUE BEAD

BYRD BAYLOR • Pictures by RONALD HIMLER

CHARLES SCRIBNER'S SONS · NEW YORK

Maxwell Macmillan Canada · Toronto
Maxwell Macmillan International
New York · Oxford · Singapore · Sydney

One small blue bead . . .
A turquoise bead
No larger than
An apple seed . . .

You might not notice
A thing so small.
You might walk by
And not see it at all
Though it shines as blue
As a piece of the sky
And bright as the flash
Of an eagle's eye.

When men still lived in cliffs and caves
And great beasts roamed the land,
There was a boy who held this bead
Clutched tightly in his hand.
Now it lies forgotten
In the desert sand.

How long has it been there?
Who can say?
Maybe ten thousand years
And one long day,
For this is a wide and lonely land
Where hardly a footstep disturbs the sand
And very few people happen to pass
A certain clump of tall dry grass
That hides this bit of blue.
But someone will find it.
Will that someone be you?

Here's a map to follow.
It's drawn to show
Where men went wandering
Ages ago.
And if it leads you to the bead
There in the sand,
Before you stoop beside it
Or take it in your hand
Look off into the desert sky,
Watch the eagles floating high,
Listen to the wind . . . and try
To let time blow away, away
Back to a dim and ancient day . . .

Back to a boy
Naked and brown in the sun.
Can't you almost see him leap?
Can't you almost see him run?
He's fast as a rabbit,
Wary as a deer.
He moves like a shadow
When danger comes near.

Yes, this is the boy
Who once stood here
Where the turquoise bead now lies.
He had no name
(Just call him Boy)
But he had dreams in his eyes.

Go back with him,
Back to a night
When cold rain was falling
And in the wind there came the whine
Of a wolf cub calling . . . calling. . . .

A band of men sat huddled in a cave
Where coals of fire glowed warm and red.
Boy lay curled on a bed of leaves
But he sat up when an old man said:

"This thought keeps spinning in my head.
There must be caves just like our own
Somewhere
And other axes made of stone
Somewhere
And other men like me."

The others only laughed.
"What foolish talk, old man.
We've been the only people
Since time began.
There are no people
Anywhere but here!"

Boy's mother blinked her eyes
In fear.
"I am afraid," she said, "to think
Of strangers coming near."

But Boy was filled with wonder.
This new thought was a thunder
In his mind.
Can there be
Far from this cave
A boy like me?

A far pale star
Fell through the night,
And the old man watched
The streak of light
That flamed and died
On the other side
Of the world.
"I want to go and see," he said.
"I want to know what's over there.
I want to wander everywhere.
I'll search for men in far-off places.
I'll touch their hands . . . I'll see their faces."

But the others said, "No,
You cannot go.
Each man here has work to do.
Who would do your share for you?"

"Not I," they said. "Not I."
"Besides," they said, "why
Should anyone want to go?
What is there to know that
We don't know?
We've found berries and seeds
To make children grow.
We've found where cold sweet waters flow.
We've learned to make a fire glow.

"Here we have shelter from wind and rain,
Here we look down on a grassy plain.
How could life be better anywhere?
Why go searching far away over there?"

The fire burned low
And still they talked
And still the men said no
And still the old man told them
How much he longed to go.

"I'll do your share.
I'll work hard and long.
And I'll try to keep you lucky
With my good-luck song."

They turned to Boy
With looks of surprise,
For he'd always been a lazy boy
With lazy laughing eyes.
If you sent him to hunt wildcats
He'd just play with butterflies.
But the boy who stood there
So straight and tall
Didn't even look like
The same boy at all.

Boy stood alone.
His words at first came shy and slow:
"I think that there is something
That just tells a man to go
In search of people who may not be,
In search of places he may not see.
Still he has to search.
That's clear to me.
Old man,
I'll tend your fire
While you're away.
I'll walk your path.
I'll hunt each day."

The others asked:
"You swear to do
The work of two?"
Boy looked at the old man,
Then he nodded his head.

"You can go where you like,
Old man," they said.
So he walked off alone,
Taking only his dreams.
The people said wisely,
"How foolish he seems."

But
Boy clambered up a hill
To watch him out of sight.
Once he smiled. Once he waved.
Then he sang with all his might.
He sang his good-luck song
To speed that old man's feet along
Like happy birds in flight.

Now Boy must do
The work of two.
His day begins while the moon still shines
And he wakes to the sound of coyote whines.
And Boy seems weak and very small
Where the storms are fierce
And the rocks are tall.
But he loves the sound
Of the wind's wild call
And he likes to crouch
On a canyon wall
Near an eagle's nest
And best of all
He likes to dream the old man's dream
Of people scattered wide.

"I wonder . . . I wonder
If on some far hillside
There is a boy
Who sits alone
And thinks the same thoughts
As my own.
I wonder if he wonders if
There's a boy with thoughts like his.
I'd like to tell him that there is
And I'm that boy."

That was a good dream,
His favorite dream, too,
But the people kept saying
It couldn't be true.
"You can search
Till the mountains disappear.
The only men you'll find
Are here!"

Let them talk. Let them talk.
Boy doesn't care.
He's too busy hunting
The fox in his lair,
And he's too busy gathering
Berries and seeds
And the roots man eats
And the stones he needs
For weapons and tools,
And he's too busy fishing
In still bright pools.

Now any time you want Boy
You have to look fast
Or he's leaping the bushes,
Flashing on past. . . .

But of all the work
He did day after day,
The hardest work was waiting for
The time to pass away.

For no old man
Came walking up the hill.
And people told Boy,
"We know he never will."

Full moons came and went.
New bees followed clover scent.
Rabbits found holes
To spend the winter in,
And Boy wrapped warm
In gray wolfskin. . . .
And summer winds came back
And filled the sky
And lifted small birds
As they learned to fly.

But no old man
Came through the mountain pass.
What sounded like his whistle
Was just wind in the grass. . . .

Now Boy heard people saying that
The tribe must wander on.
He knew then that
Hope was almost gone.
"We need a wide new hunting ground,
Some far valley where we'll hear the sound
Of mammoths trumpeting in the night—
Where the sky is full of birds
And bison roam in herds
And the fish in the lake flash bright."

They all said, "Yes,
For our hunters bring home
Less and less. . . .
We must move on."

Boy said, "How will the old man
Ever guess
Which way through all the wilderness
We have gone?"

"Forget him, Boy.
We must move on.
We'll be gone
When the first
Light of dawn
Touches the sky."

Boy didn't argue.
Boy didn't cry.
But just one last time
He thought he would climb
His favorite hill
And see what clouds
Were drifting by
And sit there quiet and still
Just this one last time. . . .

But look! There by those faraway trees
Something moves. Is it only the shadows Boy sees?
He shades his eyes. It moves again.
You'd almost think it was—TWO MEN!
His heart beats fast. He squints at the sun.
"MEN!" he shouts. "MEN!"
And he wants to run,
To call, to wave—
To bring them up the hill to the cave.

But the others cry, "Danger!"
Their eyes show fear.
"There cannot be people
Except right here."
Now they gather up boulders,
Each man has a spear,
And they wait on the mountain
Where the cliffs are sheer.
"Will there be others at their side?"
"Shall we fight or shall we hide?"

But Boy said, "No,
Whoever they are
We must welcome our brothers,
For they have walked far
Just as we have walked before
And soon will walk again.
Perhaps they, too, have wondered
If they were the only men."

The people stood watching
As the figures grew.
Boy saw their faces.
And one he knew.

Suddenly
The old man's whistle
Was heard.

To Boy it sounded gayer
Than a singing bird
Could ever sound.
He whirled around
And ran in a flurry
Of dust and joy
To the place where
The old man stood—
With a boy.

He was skinny and brown,
Just about Boy's size
With just about the same kind
Of dreams in his eyes.

They stared in silence
A little while.
Boy lowered his eyes
Then tried to smile.

People gazed at this new boy
And even touched his hand.
They shook their heads as though it were
Too much to understand.

Boy said, "Did you ever wonder
If there were other boys like you?"
"Yes, I used to wonder that."
"Well, I did, too."

And they gathered there in silence
And listened to him tell
Of wonders like a roaring sea
And the sound in one seashell
And deserts where no drop of rain
Ever fell.
He had seen drawings scratched in rock,
Needles made of bone,
Red and yellow paint,
Points and knives of stone
And here and there
Restless roaming bands
Of men who walk the wide
And lonely land. . . .

Around his neck
The new boy wore
Something they never had
Seen before—
It was tied with a reed,
One small blue bead,
A turquoise bead,
No larger than
An apple seed.

He said to Boy,
"This is for you.
Did you ever see
A blue so blue?
Look how it holds
The color of the sky.
It's like a flower
That will never die."

Boy took the bead
And held it tight
And looked at it
In every light
And said, "I'll wear it
Day and night.

"And I'll never feel
Alone again,
For any good thing
Can happen when
The world is full of
Tribes of men
Who know that they have brothers.
The bead reminds me of those others
Everywhere.
It makes me dare
Wonderful things
And my heart sings
My good-luck song. . . ."

And soon enough
His song was heard
On many a
Misty hilltop
By many a
Startled bird,
For the tribe set out
At the break of day—
Boy, and the old man,
Leading the way.

They passed by nameless canyons
And saw nameless rivers flow.
They followed mountain ridges
Into the valleys below.
And the way was
Rocky
And hard
And slow,
For that's the only way
The tribe of men could go
In that distant time
When Boy went walking
Across this land,
Holding a blue bead
In his hand. . . .

Now the blue bead lies
In a sandy place
Where the winter weeds
All look like lace
And a gopher sits
With the sun in his face,
Looking out over the desert land
While eagles drop shadows
On the white hot sand.

If you find it please take care
Not to leave it just anywhere,
For the boy named Boy
Would be happy to know
That his bead goes with you
Wherever you go. . . .